When Prayers Go Up
Blessings Rain Down

Written by: Christopher C. Smith

2

Christopher C. Smith

Father, Author, Actor, Song Writer, Independent Book & Movie Publisher

Thank you's & Dedications

First I would like to give thanks to God

My Beautiful Mother
Ora Henderson

My Beautiful Daughter
Lauren Madison Smith

My Supportive A.O.D Family

My Beautiful sister Valerie Hayes, My niece Valyn My nephews Vashon and D.J., Cash Blocka. My Canada family, Darrell Washington , Bugs Money & Jocelyn, Yeti, Berea, Anghellic & The Entire Rios Family, Jesus Kontroverse Ortiz, Ryan Levin & 4sure ent. Shacora Johnson, My Entire Philly Family, My whole Yonkers & Bronx Family, Cas YoungStar, Curly Jay & My Entire Miami Family, Moe Dirdee, Nikki & Amy, My whole Detroit Family, Robert Jackson & Every Body at the Wal-Mart #5404 Store, DJ Antonio and the wonderful Staff at Wal-Mart Radio !!!

Sponsored By

Ryan Levin & 4 Sure Ent.

Contact Info: Ryan@4suredjs.com

&
Darrell Washington

Contact by Email : Contact@famlyinc.com

The Prelude

"Aubrey!" my dad yelled. The tone of his voice shattered my sleep. For some reason, I felt as though today wasn't going to be my day.

"Come on now we don't have all day! We're going to be late for your aunt's funeral" he said repeatedly.

I hate going to funerals, I thought to myself.

The emotions and tension from different family members make the whole event kind of awkward.

I started getting dressed, and while pulling up my pants I couldn't help but reminisce about the good times my aunt (Who shared the same name as me), and I had.

It's crazy what drugs can do to a person. It can alter someone life.

"Hey dad," I said with a serious look on my face, "can you promise that when we get there, I will not have to speak to my mom knowing she walked out of my life when I was months old and haven't seen her in about seven years"?

"Ok Aubrey, just hurry up and let's get ready to go. I'm trying not to be late. I want to get a good seat at least" my dad replied with a slight smirk on his face.

I was done with my hair. We were out of the house, and in less than a minute my life changed for the worse.

The sound of sirens from police cars and the helicopters that filled my lawn left a sudden shock on my face. I didn't know what was going on or what to expect.

"You! Get on the ground now you're under arrest." One of the officers said while yelling at the top of his voice.

"What's going on?" asked dad looking confused and disturbed about the situation.

Tears willfully rolled down my cheeks as I saw my dad get arrested and placed in the back seat of the car.

As my dad was driven away, a lady with a long dress came to me explaining that I was going to be taken to the group home.

Chapter 1

As I sat in my room, still in shock of the arrest, I wondered how I'd survive in the group home for a couple of months with all the different types of teens who seemed cool for the most part.

Listening to some of their stories makes my situation not even worth a complaint.

"Hey, you did you hear the announcement right? Everyone is to stay in the day room. We are doing a head count this morning to make sure everyone is here." One of the staffs said, peeping into my room. As I looked up to see who peeped, one of the staff members brown eyes and cute smile caught my attention.

"Ok!" I replied. As I made my way to the day room, the butterflies in my stomach started to grow more and more.

While our names were called, I noticed and felt the tension from this particular female and I tried not to make it obvious that I saw her staring at me with my head held low.

I immediately lift my head on hearing the voice of the young man that pulled me from my room.

"Hi, my name is Alex Hunter, and I'm your new dorm leader/instructor and..."

As he began to speak, he was shortly interrupted by the girl who was just staring at me.

"Um, what happened to our last instructor?" She said with a slight simper on her face.

"Well I was going to get into that before I was rudely interrupted." he quickly answered and then continued.

"As I said before, my name is Alex or simply call me Mr. Hunter."

With his hands demonstrating his speech, he continued "I know you young ladies are used to having this place run in a certain way, but a little of that is going to change. One thing I will not tolerate is disrespect. We must treat each other the same way we will like to be treated. We will start doing chores around here at the beginning of the week, and by the end of the week you all will be rewarded."

I could tell by the tone of his voice he was not joking.

"Rewarded,'
What kind of reward?" the same girl interrupted Mr. Hunter again and this time with more attention from the other teens who were giggling.

"Why don't you stand up, introduce yourself and tell us a little bit about you." Mr. Hunter replied.

She stood up after rolling her eyes and snapping her neck and said: "well umm my name is Desiree and I'm here because my parents are drug addicts and no family member wanted to take me in."

With her arms folded and neck twirling for what seemed like the hundredth time, I couldn't help but feel sorry for her. As the meeting went on, we were called one after the other to introduce ourselves and tell the story of how we ended up here.

The chores were given out with Desiree and myself ending up with the bathroom duties. "this can't be bad," I thought to myself.

While making my way back to the room, I felt a light push. I turned around and found out that it was Desiree.

I was about to introduce myself when she aggressively interrupted me with the rest of her click surrounding me. Desiree spoke in words that seem like a threat. "I've seen you eye and blush over the new instructor. He is off limits. He is all mine. So, if I see or even hear about you getting close to him, then it's going to be me and you." she warned.

Before I could even reply her, she walked off with her friends. I walked into my room and found my new roommate.

"Hi my name is Mya, and I'm a neat freak," she said while giggling. "Why are you here?" she asked with a strange look on her face.

"Hi...," I started to introduce myself when I noticed Desiree and her girls staring at me through the window.

I took a deep breath and then began to tell my new roommate the issues I had encountered and how I ended up here.

"Well, I see you packed a lot, so you must be here for a long time," Mya said in a sarcastic tone.

I explained to Mya that I had to speak with the worker I was handed to and get an update on my dad's case and see where it all goes from here.

Excited Mya went on telling me how being a neat freak made it impossible for her to keep a roommate for so long.

She had been there for five years since she lost her parents in an auto crash and had gone through at least 25 different roommates in that span of time.

After going on for about 45 minutes, she then begins to whisper, asking whether I am yet to hear any rumor about what has been going on in the group homes.

With a confused look on my face "No, what stories?"

I asked in a very concerned voice.

While taking a walk around the premises, she pointed out who and where the mischievous people and places were and the people I shouldn't be hanging out with.

As we went on, someone tapped my shoulder. I found out it was Alex. He wanted to know how we were doing and to be sure we weren't getting into any trouble.

Oh no! Those butterflies were back in my stomach. I tried to hide my red face, but he noticed I was blushing and began to smile as if he knew how I felt.

"Well, it's almost time for you to lay it down. You have school in the morning." Alex said and started to walk away.

As Alex took few steps away from us, another staff worker came up to introduce himself. "Oh wow," he said as he hastily grabbed my hand and gently kissed it and introduced himself as Jonathan.

"What's yours?" he asked. I wasn't done introducing myself when he already had a textbook of questions for me.

The few seconds he spent questioning me, I could tell Jonathan was really into me. Alex stopped to look at us, but his facial expression wasn't good at all.

Mya couldn't help but giggle through everything that had happened.

I think she knew what was going on.

We said our goodbyes and walked back into our room.

Chapter 2

Ring! Ring!! Ring!!! My alarm went off. I quickly jumped out of bed to get ready for the school program the group home had to offer when I noticed that Mya was already up and was getting ready. "Come on girl; we don't have all day! We have chores to do before making our way to school," she said emphatically.

After slugging around and taking my time, I finally got ready when I heard a knock on the door. It was one of the staff members, Jonathan. I had to report to my counselor's office before going to class.

I asked if everything was ok or if I was in some trouble.

"I have no idea" he replied before offering to take me to the office as I didn't know my way. As we made our way through the building, Jonathan stopped me, and with a serious look on his face told me that he was attracted to me.

"Truthfully," I replied, "you are very handsome, but I am going through a lot right now. However, let's see where this takes us."

"How I wish it were Alex making his confessions to me," I thought to myself.

As the conversation went on, I found myself walking into what seemed like my counselor's room.

"Hi! Aubrey. I have a message from your father. He is being charged with theft, but he pleaded not guilty. Your dad said his lawyers are on the case and are trying to overturn it. He maintains that it's a case of mistaken identity."

With a concerned face, the counselor continued; "he said you should sit still and hold your head up as you'd be spending a couple of months or more with us."

With tears in my eyes, I held my head down, slowly shaking it.

"Are you ok?" the counselor asked.

"yes, I'm fine sir." But I didn't get to do my chore. Will I be in trouble?" I asked nervously.

"No, you won't. I'm pretty sure John or Alex will understand." answered the Counselor.

I tried to hold back from crying and started to make my way towards my class. Desiree and her friends were also in the same class.

Shortly after taking my seat, the girls started whispering to each other.

Surprisingly, yet gracefully, Alex walked in. He was our teacher. We locked eyes with each other, and I received this chilling wink from him. The whole of my body system sparked up.

"Well, what is it that you don't do?" Desiree loudly said as if she was trying to crack a joke, shattering my moment of bliss.

With the quickest and slickest comeback, Alex replied: "fall for you." The entire class went up in an uproar with laughter as Desiree's face charged up in anger.

The class went on fine until Desiree and friends decided to interrupt the class. They began to laugh aimlessly and so loud. She felt the need to make a comeback.

"Well, what's so funny?" asked Alex with a serious look on his face.

The two began to argue, and Alex suddenly shouted, "get out of my class," pointing at the classroom door.

"Fine! The class is over anyway" Desiree exclaimed. The bell rang minutes later.

The class was over. The day went by so fast. We were leaving the classroom when I saw Jonathan waiting outside alone with his hands behind him. "What's up? How was your day?" he asked sweetly, holding up a couple of roses he was apparently hiding behind him.

"Aww! Thanks so much " I said as my heart began to melt. I could honestly say I was falling for Jonathan a little more than I was for Alex.

"Let's go to the cafeteria and eat" he suggested because I was new to the group home that I couldn't leave just yet due to the fact I was still on my 90-day probation.

"That's fine" I replied, knowing how hungry I was. We had only taken few steps when I felt sharp pains. I thought less of it. "I probably rubbed up against something and didn't notice," I thought silently. I was so hungry, and I just wanted to eat, so I cared less.

As we sat to eat, we told our personal stories to each other. John also shared with me how he ended up working there.

After spending time with John, I started to feel something that could be more than a friendship, but that wasn't the only feeling at that point. The sharp pains were back and worse.

Chapter 3

"I barely see you since you and John been hanging out so much. Let's go and chill somewhere" Mya said in a joking tone.

"But Mya," I said, "I noticed all the crazy things you warned me about are true; ranging from girls doing things for special favors, to the male staff members harassing and pushing themselves upon innocent girls."

I knew I had to do something before the moral decadence from the male staff members oozes up to me. Days went by with Mya and myself getting closer, hanging out, playing board games and telling each other our deepest secrets, the sharp pains also persisted. Also, I was stuck in between John and Alex but also didn't want to get into any trouble knowing that I would only be here until my dad's case is sorted out.

"Hey Aubrey," Mya said with an outburst of excitement. "we should attend the party going on at the other side of the building close to the auditorium if you are bored."

With a bit of hesitation, I quickly took the offer without asking any questions. There was nothing else to do.

We dolled ourselves up and headed out. As we got closer to the party, we could hear the loud music and people screaming and singing along.

But, for some reasons, I still couldn't shake the achiness and fatigue I been feeling as of late. We finally made our way to the party arena but got a little worried and nervous seeing that there were drugs and alcohol in the room and a lot of making out in the hallway.

"What's wrong?" Mya gently whispered in my ear. "You've never been to a party like this before?" With no hesitation, I replied, "No, my father would have killed me had I been caught just several feet away from a party like this." Daddy's little girl, he isn't here, is he?" Mya said, teasing me. "Shake it up girl," she commanded. "Ease up, come in here and have a good time. You'll forget all your worries and stress."

I took a deep breath and made my way into the room, but I felt so out of place deep down and was ready to go back to my room to sleep.

But Mya quickly grabbed my hand, and I knew for a fact that I couldn't leave just yet.

With the room that is halfway dark, I could barely see who was there or see any known person.

I tried to join the band by leaning against the wall, trying my hardest not to feel so out of place. I couldn't dance if it were to save my life, so quickly I started nodding my head. Suddenly, a group of guys came walking towards our way.

"Hey, would you pretty women like to dance?" one of the guys asked. I quickly had a flashback of a ballroom dancing which I am used to, but the type of music being played in that party did no justice. It wasn't that type of party.

I declined the offer while Mya, with the brightest smile on her face, quickly accepted

I found my way to an empty seat but the request to dance, smoke or drink never ceased.

I turned down each of those requests,

But my method of answering got even worse as the night passed. I was tired and bored.

Mya, on the other hand, was hyperactive and every time a new song came on, she was asked to dance.

My phone became my companion.

Eventually, my phone battery was running low, and I needed to charge it. I got up to look for a socket to plug my phone when John tapped my shoulder.

"What's up and what are you doing here?" he asked with a slightly concerned look on his face.

"I was dragged down here by my friend-slash-roommate who had asked me to come with her because she didn't want to be left alone."

"But what are you doing here?" I asked.

"The same thing you are doing here, I'm with Alex. We were bored and decided to see if the loud commotion could do justice to our boredom."

As our conversation continued, I started to feel nauseous. I didn't want to throw up in the party or worse still, at John. So, I quickly asked him to accompany me to the washroom.

The more steps we took the heavier and tired I became. I then leaned on the hallway walls.

"Are you ok?" John asked in a serious tone "what would you like me to do?"

Just as I tried to answer, we got to the restroom, but the door was locked.

We both turned to look at each other with a confused look on our face while we tried knocking a couple of time and asking if anyone was in there.

There were movements in the washroom, but no one was saying anything.

"Hold on. You are knocking too softly. You got to knock much harder." John said jokingly

John banged on the door, demanding that the door is opened because there was an emergency and that he was going to call the cops if they refuse to open the door.

Some seconds later, the doorknob turned, and the door opened. It was Alex, half-naked, rushing to put his clothes on and right behind him was Desiree- the girl who had a problem with me since day one.

Tears slowly filled my eyes, and my heart began to break into pieces slowly. I forgot the reason why I headed to the bathroom in the first place.

Alex who didn't see me went on to argue with and yell at John for knocking on the door.

The two begin to argue because Alex could lose his job had the company found out he was sleeping with students of the group home. That was something they took serious knowing the fact that 95 percent of the teens there were underage.

I didn't know if I should comment or not. I still had feelings for Alex even though I was talking to John, but I never let him know.

As the arguing got more and more intense, I showed my face so that Alex would know that the reason John was knocking on the door was so that I could use the restroom.

Our eyes locked and tears rolled down my cheeks. Everything had come to a complete stop between Alex and I because I knew deep down he had felt something for me just as much as I had.

"Excuse me! Let me out of here. You can make up sometime

later; I'm headed back to the party" Desiree cut into my thoughts.

As she made her way out the washroom with a slight giggle and smirk on her face, she noticed me and stopped.

With her arms crossed while rolling her eyes, she said: "oh, it's you again."

I tried my best not to let the anger I felt overcome me.

I took a deep breath and replied, "Yeah, it's me. What smart thing you got to say now?"

I came on my guard in case she wanted to try something. She took a step back, and I had a feeling she was going to try something dumb.

Within seconds, she swung grazed her punched in my face.

I quickly moved back, and with all the anger and hatred I was holding back, I jumped towards her in an aggressive uproar.

She stumbled to the floor.

"Help!" she cried. "Get her off me," she repeatedly yelled at her hair, clothes, and blood was all over me.

John and Alex started to pull me off of her yelling, "Let her go, let her go."

Before I knew it, there was a huge crowd around us. With a few of the other teens filming videos and taking pictures of the awful sight, I created with their phones.

After a few minutes of trying to get me to release my hand from her hair, Alex was finally successful. I heard the police sirens.

One of the cops then rushed through the screaming "break it up, break it up."

He drew his gun, and everyone scattered. He then pointed the gun at us; we also began to scream.

It was John who stood up to the officer who seemed not to know what exactly was going on.

I then yelled, "Just let it go John."

The cop wasn't trying to hear any of it, even though Alex was trying to explain. All he knew was that he got a call that there was a crowd in the hallway and teens were fighting.

With the officer's gun still out and pointed at John as if he was the cause of the commotion, himself and Alex asked the cop to put the gun away and that he was scaring everyone.

The cop looked as though he was not trying to hear any of that even with Desiree and me both crying on the floor out of fear.

The first thing he saw was Desiree's hair and blood everywhere, and he grew angrier. John who noticed the officer's temper had changed for the worst, grabbed the gun and the two started to tussle

Alex, Desiree and I could only watch out of fear as a couple of shots were let off into the hallway ceiling, causing some of the tile and fixtures to fall to the ground everywhere.

"Stop, stop" we all yelled as tears fell from our cheeks even harder.

Suddenly the gun fell out their hands and next to my feet. I quickly grabbed the arm and pointed at them.

"Stop!" I yelled at the top of my lungs as I cried even harder. I wanted to say more, but my body won't allow. I had forgotten that I was in much pain.

I fell back on the ground hitting my head on some of the rebels that had fallen from the ceiling and fainted.

Chapter 4

"Hey you," I heard as I slowly regained consciousness.

To my surprise, it was Alex' voice I heard. He then went on about how I had fainted and had been rushed to the nearby hospital and was hooked up to a lot of machines.

"I'm sorry," he said as he gently grabbed my hands. "From the first time I saw you, I felt deeply in love but was too shy and nervous to say anything to you. But then I saw you on a couple of occasions with John, and I automatically assumed you guys were a couple."

Slowly wiping the tears from my eyes, I agreed as I then told him how I genuinely felt. But I also said to him that John and I talked but decided on taking things slow because of my age.

I took the opportunity to ask him what he was doing in the bathroom with Desiree half naked. I could tell I hit a sharp nerve as he went on about how the staffs at the group home have sex with the girls for pleasure and special treatments.

Different thoughts ran through my mind as his reply left me dumbfounded.

I wanted to give him a response when the doctor walked in. With paperwork and a clipboard,

I assumed he was going to tell me that I was ok and that he would send me on my way.

Instead, he looked down at his clipboard and strolled through a couple of pages took a deep breath, opened his mouth and said, "Miss. Williams,

I'm sorry you have leukemia."

"What," I said in a shaky voice as tears rolled down my face rapidly.

"Looking at the X-rays, you have what we called Acute Myeloid Leukemia -AML." The doctor said quickly.

"What is that?" I said, shaking my head.

"AML is the most prevalent of all acute leukemia.

It occurs when the bone marrow begins to make blasts when cells are not completely matured.

These blasts usually develop into white blood cells. However, in AML, these cells do not grow and are unable to prevent infections.

In AML, the red blood cells and platelets may become abnormal because of the bone marrow. These abnormal cells increase rapidly, and the unusual leukemia cells begin to crowd out the healthy white blood and red blood cells, and platelets that the body needs.

Based on the cell that leukemia developed, one of the main things that differentiate AML from the other primary forms of leukemia is its eight different subtypes.

I was so lost and clueless about the entire jargon the doctor said. So, I asked, "Will I be ok?"

"Yes!" the Doctor replied, "luckily, we were able to catch it early, so nothing major is going to be done but some chemotherapy. We'll give you a combination of drugs that will destroy as many leukemia cells as possible and bring your blood counts to normal. This will be followed by consolidation chemotherapy, to destroy any remaining leukemia cells that cannot be seen in the blood or bone marrow, so we might need you to stay a lot longer than you might have wanted to."

"That will mean surgery, right?" I asked the doctor, still crying.

"Yes," the doctor replied.

My staff and I are taking it very seriously and are scheduling you for the first open slot we have so that nothing worse comes from this.

Shortly after, I was wheeled to the surgery room. I began saying the prayers my dad had taught me to say whenever I'm faced with tough times.

Knowing things could've been worse, I was glad that through all of this, Alex was still by my side holding my hands.

I said my prayers and wished it was all a dream as I was laid on the operating table and put to sleep.

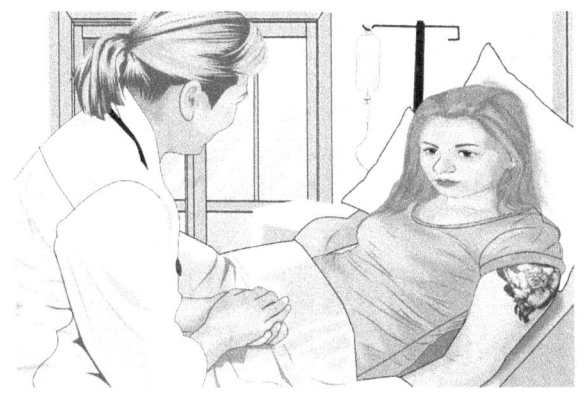

Chapter 5

"Wake up dear," I heard a nurse say. I opened my eyes to look at the nurse, but the sun ray peeping through the blinds kept my eyes shut. "Shut the blinds, shut the blinds," I repeatedly said while laughing. "I'm still alive," I said again, joyfully.

"Yes, you are…" John said softly, leaning towards me. I think I had the widest smile ever. "Guess what today is?" he asked happily. He reminded me that it was my 18th birthday.

John then invited the rest of the staff members to celebrate with me. Desiree was also part of them. She kept apologizing.

I calmly said to her "It's ok, I forgive you." We hugged and cried together.

The nurses also handed me some flowers and balloons. I was touched

"That's not all Aubrey," John said. He then removed the curtain that was separating me from my other roommate. It was my dad!

I couldn't control the tears any longer. We hugged each other tightly.

"When did you get out," I asked as I tried my hardest to remain composed.

"Earlier today," he replied. The judge was presented with evidence, and I was let go. I had got the word about all that has been happening, and I'm so sorry that you had to go through all of this."

As the day passed, I began to ruminate how blessed I am indeed, and all I could say is "When prayers go up blessings rain down!"

THE END!

Inspired By:

Zack "Yeti" Strain

Berea Snow

D.J. Buddy Finch

Robert R. Jackson

In A Heart Felt Memory Of

Sun Rise
12/11/95

Sun Set
2/13/18

Cristian Barajas-Grimaldo